Grandude's Green Submarine

Dear Reader,

Do you like adventures?

My name is Edward Marshall Sr. But my grandchildren call me Grandude, and they are my Chillers—Lucy, Tom, Em, and Bob. We love to go on magical adventures together. And this is the story of our journey to find another very special adventurer—why don't you come along for the ride!

Yours sincerely,

Grandude

To my own chillers with love—P.M.

For my family—K.D.

Visit us on the Web! rhcbooks.com

Educators and librarians, for a variety of teaching tools, visit us at RHTeachersLibrarians.com

Library of Congress Cataloging-in-Publication Data is available upon request.
ISBN 978-0-593-37243-2 (trade)
ISBN 978-0-593-37244-9 (lib. bdg.)
ISBN 978-0-593-37245-6 (ebook)

Jacket art and interior illustrations by Kathryn Durst
MANUFACTURED IN CHINA
10 9 8 7 6 5 4 3 2 1
First Edition

Grandude's Green Submarine

Written by
Paul McCartney

Illustrated by
Kathryn Durst

Random House 🏠 New York

It was a BOILING hot summer's day.

Em

Lucy

"TOO HOT!" said Tom.

Tom

Bob

And the other Chillers—Lucy, Em, and Bob—all agreed.

Grandude peeped out from his garden shed.
"Too hot for you, is it? Come inside."

"Welcome to my top-secret **Inventions Shed!**" said Grandude.

It was as cool as an iced drink (or an ice rink)—full of unusual cooling devices. And all sorts of other mysterious creations, too.

As the Chillers explored, Lucy spotted a picture of Nandude, their adventurous grandmother.

Grandude's eyes sparkled. "I think she loves adventures even more than I do!"

"When will we see her again?" asked Bob.
"Perhaps *we* could go on an adventure to find her!" said Em.

"Great minds think alike," said Grandude.
"And I have a plan. . . .

"Follow me!"

Grandude led the children down a secret
passageway until they reached a locked door.

"This is my favorite invention yet," Grandude said,
opening the door to reveal . . .

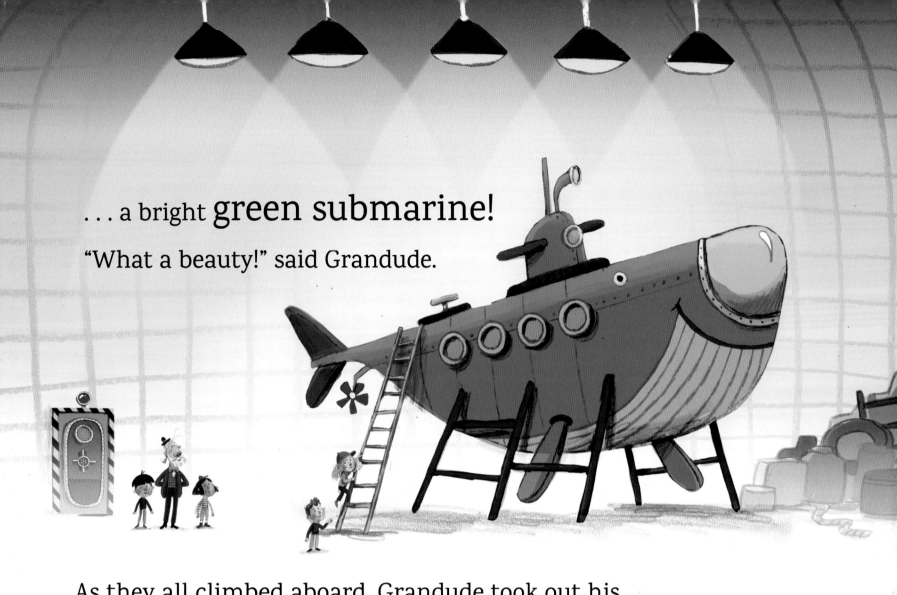

. . . a bright **green submarine!**

"What a beauty!" said Grandude.

As they all climbed aboard, Grandude took out his
golden magic compass from his trouser pocket.

"We'll need a bit of magic to get started.
This is no ordinary sub, you know!"

Magic needle spinning 'round,
lift this green sub off the ground.

With a **Zing, bang, Sizzle,** the green submarine jerked and jolted, then sprang up into the air and shot through the roof of the shed!

The Chillers laughed and cheered as they zoomed up into the clouds.

"We're swimming through the sky," said Em.

"I think I know who might be able to help us find Nandude," said Grandude as they flew along, singing songs and watching the world far below.

"We're nearly there, Chillers,"
cried Grandude as the submarine flew
down through heavy rain-filled clouds.

"Hold on tight!"

They went whirling
and bumping and spiraling down,

down,

down . . .

landing at the edge of a little village.

"Hey, Grandude!" shouted a man on a big white stallion, smiling and waving furiously.

"We're just where we need to be," said Grandude. "Meet my friend Ravi."

"And you're just in time for the parade," said Ravi.

Ravi took Grandude and the Chillers to a shady terrace. It was the perfect spot to watch the parade while Grandude and Ravi told stories about Nandude's adventures.

"Nandude taught me this tune," said Ravi, strumming his sitar. "If you want to find her, just follow the notes. And watch how it makes the animals sing and dance!"

But as they listened, another sound started.

Drip, drop, plip, plop—the rain had come.

"Oh no!" said Bob. "The storm has found us!"

"We won't be able to fly through a **monsoon!**" said Tom as the rain poured down.

"Don't worry," said Grandude. "We won't need to fly. Quick, Chillers! **Catch that sub!**"

The green submarine was floating away on the rising rainwater!

They all hopped aboard the submarine
just in time. Ravi waved goodbye as the
current sent them swooshing down the river. . . .

"Where is the river taking us, Grandude?" asked Lucy.

"I have a notion we're heading for the ocean!" said Grandude.

As the river rushed them through a lush jungle, they heard a familiar tune. . . .

The animals on the riverside were all singing snatches
of Nandude's song!

They passed **tigers** and **toucans**,

and **birds** and **baboons**,

leopards and **lemurs**,

warthogs and **bullfrogs**.

"If we follow the music, we're sure to find her!" said Bob.
The river widened and they reached its mouth. . . .

And then the green submarine began to dive down

deep,

deep,

deep

into the shimmering blue ocean.

Deeper and deeper they went,
cruising past the most spectacular sea life.

Grandude happily pointed out dolphins, sharks,
and whales, who all seemed excited to see him.

But all of a sudden there was a jolt,
and everything went dark!

They were caught in the tentacles of
a giant OCTOPUS spraying clouds
of jet-black ink.

It was so dark that Grandude couldn't find his magic compass—
and even he was getting a little bit worried.

"What's that sound?" asked Bob nervously.

"It's that tune
we heard before—
Nandude's MUSIC!
And it's getting louder,"
said Grandude.

Louder . . .
    and BRIGHTER!

Each note lit up the sea
in a magical light show.

It was Nandude!

Her huge underwater ship was sailing toward them.

As the ship approached, the octopus began to dance.
And as it danced, it let go of the green submarine.
Grandude and the Chillers were free!

Other sea creatures joined the octopus's wild dance.

And meanwhile a trail of magical music from
Nandude's ship scooped up the green submarine . . .

. . . and carried it out of the sea and into the sky.

They sailed through the air, over sea and land. All the way back . . .

. . . to Grandude's garden!

One of the accordionship's
windows creaked open. . . .

"Hey, Nandude!"

Grandude and the Chillers waved
as Nandude climbed down from the ship.

"Nandude to the rescue!" she said with a wink,
giving them all a big hug.

"Goodness me, you've all grown up so much." Nandude sounded
a bit worried. "I must have been away far longer than I thought!"

"After all that, I think it's time
for some tea and biscuits," said Grandude.

As they got cozy in the living room,
Nandude told them all about her adventures.

And then it was time for bed. Nandude played lullabies on her accordion while the Chillers snuggled down.

"Maybe we can go on an adventure with you, Nandude," Tom said with a yawn.

"Yes, maybe we can do that someday," she whispered. "That would be fun! Now, off to sleep you go."

Nandude and Grandude kissed the Chillers good night,
and pretty soon they were fast asleep.

Nandude turned and smiled at Grandude—
but he was asleep, too!

Sleep tight, Chillers.
Sleep tight, Grandude.